"The poetry of Rane Arroyo is in your face and visionary at the same time. His delicious and sly use of language makes for great irony, humor, and sadness. His Singing Shark is an earthy trickster who swims this dark sea of America, tearing freely at the bland, white buttocks of intolerance and ignorance. Bravo!"   —Adrian C. Louis

"An important and long-awaited addition to U.S. Puerto Rican/Latino literature and to contemporary poetry in general . . . deeply felt vital personal/collective experience turned into impeccable, exhilarating tours de force by an implacable wit, a generous, original talent and a vast knowledge of the art of poetry . . ."
                          —Carlos A. Rodríguez Matos

". . . the poems in their ironic expression and wit feel like the bite of a shark that will always surprise, shock, and hunt the reader . . ."   —Alberto Sandoval

"A spoof, a celebration, a lament, a euphoric ride."
                          —Toi Derricotte

Bilingual Press/Editorial Bilingüe

General Editor
   Gary D. Keller

Managing Editor
   Karen S. Van Hooft

Associate Editors
   Karen M. Akins
   Barbara H. Firooyze

Assistant Editor
   Linda St. George Thurston

Editorial Board
   Juan Goytisolo
   Francisco Jiménez
   Eduardo Rivera
   Mario Vargas Llosa

Address:
Bilingual Press
Hispanic Research Center
Arizona State University
P.O. Box 872702
Tempe, Arizona 85287-2702
(602) 965-3867

The SINGING SHARK

RANE ARROYO

Bilingual Press/Editorial Bilingüe
TEMPE, ARIZONA

ISBN 0-927534-61-4

Library of Congress Cataloging-in-Publication Data

Arroyo, Rane.
    The singing shark / Rane Arroyo.
        p. cm.
    ISBN 0-927534-61-4   (alk. paper)
    I. Title.
PS3551.R722S57   1996
811'.54–dc20   96-14356
                                         CIP

PRINTED IN THE UNITED STATES OF AMERICA

Cover design by Bidlack Creative Services

Cover art from The Atlantis Southwest Series by Gilbert Durán

Back cover photo by Scott Stoner

Acknowledgments

I'm grateful to my editors and readers for their time investments in my work. Some poems in this book have appeared in earlier versions in:

Amelia, Another Chicago Magazine, Apalachee Quarterly, Bottom-fish, Callaloo, Chants, Crucible, Hammers, Heaven Bone, Hyphen, Jeopardy, Kaleidoscope Ink, Kenyon Review, The Ledge, Mangrove, Owen Wister Review, Pennsylvania Review, Poetpourri, Postmodern Syndrome, Raven Chronicles, RiverSedge, Sacrifice the Common Good, and *Sonora Review.*

Some of the poems of Section II comprised *The Red Bed*, the 1993 Sonora Review National Chapbook Winner (Univ. of Arizona Press).

"Juan Angel" was published in the anthology *For A Living* (University of Illinois Press).

"The Carlos Poems" (The First Visit) won 2nd place in the 1992 Allen Ginsberg National Poetry Contest.

CONTENTS

*for Glenn and Diva
and for the sisters, Little Bee and Anita Josefina;*

*and I remember you:
Uncle Rachel, Cousin Jimmy Fernández, and that stranger,
Reinaldo Arenas;*

and San Carlos, someone still loves you

1

THE POSTMODERN PUEBLO

> They become kindred spirits
> in a land overflowing with ghosts. Kindred spirits in a dying
> sun's world.
> —Adrian C. Louis

ÁNGEL AMONG THE ANGELS

Tale One

The United States was
merely news reels to me,

grainy and graying.
My school friends wanted

to see my pet burros.
They were in my attic,

but they only gave rides
to the naked and the dead.

Sometimes the burros showed up
on coffee commercials

only to end up as meals
for unexpected guests.

Tale Two

One Halloween I went as a white boy.
I stuffed my crotch with gym socks.

"Why aren't you in disguise?" they asked me.
They were ghosts. White on white,

Frosty the Snowman's children, architects
inspired by the bone's long but vulnerable lines.

My friends shared one secret:
how to be at the center of the universe.

They would have been scared not to be that.
Imagine that, I reported to my black cat.

I ate candy, wondering which uncle picked
the cane for this festival of sugar.

Tale Three

Papi called moths
the poor people's angels,

but even they
got away from me.

I watched them make
the horizon an illusion,

a burning world in
which any rain storm

tore holes
inside my head.

Then darkness
would spill

out of me as if
I were Satan's piñata.

Tale Four

The universe is shaped like a sombrero,
and my taco is your taco, señor.

When I was young, I was old.
That's how it was and still is.

MULTILINGUAL SILENCES

1.

The Attic is
a Mexican restaurant.
It's passing.
Reread your Langston Hughes.

2.

My black bean soup is a cup
of a Caribbean night.
I will not spend it making love
or in worshipping sharks
on a nude beach in moonlight.
To be accused of romanticism
is to receive a fist in your face
without the grace of the blow back.

3.

I order
my Tex-Mex
meal in English
from a white
economics
major who
shrugs when
I offer
my gold
American Express
and of course
a Latino
washes my plate.

LONELINESS IN PUERTO RICO

This mango reminds me of childhood's
Adam—eating and dreaming at will.

An electrician hangs outside of
my window. Jesus, he's stripping!

Oh, it's you, Señor Sun! You're old news.
While I eat the mango, it grows dark.

BLUE COUSIN

I walk past the Pleasure Chest in whose windows
two Teddy bears in leather whip the hell
out of each other. Yeah, I laugh. If I

don't, I might get hauled away for crying
on Broadway, far from Vietnam. A bar
for a church. Jukebox pickpockets the sex

life out of me. Yes, I can Watusi.
Mama Cass, this is dedicated to me:
I was once a virgin and unloved.

America, my crotch had a future
in it. I was just 17, in wet
underwear, shooting at the North Star, New Year's

day. In the army, I learned that body
bags are for corpses. Ghosts have to hitchhike.
My tattoos are scars made beautiful.

Mateo Is Turning into a Piñata Tonight

She asked me in a Jackie O voice
to dye my Che-curly hair
blonde so she could be
haunted by a capitalist
in a Beach Boys' song.

I didn't even do that for her:
she who swam naked with me.
That seems important now.
As do these questions:

Why does the man in the moon
have only a head?

Why doesn't my semen
ever dry into a treasure map?

COURTYARD MEDITATION

Sunlight, in its own
way, rusts a house, its
windows and doors, its
inhabitants, but still
the young man takes
his Costa Rican coffee to
the courtyard and dares
think about thinking
about some lover whose
body has grown less
material than the fact
it once filled up a night
as an idea, an argument
of muscle and mystery.

> *(The unmarried daughter across the way is pushed to
> dust the statue next to this man, but as always, her
> luck is bad for the statue honors a notorious colonial
> cardinal who used Indian skulls as paperweights.
> She blushes before a lover never to be hers and
> covers the statue's exposed sex with her hands,
> ancient figleaves. The young man and girl age far
> away from each other's eyes.)*

ARTURO

Today, I'm just like a cockroach squirming
between morning's pinched blue fingers.
News in this New Age: another government falls.

Another ex-lover sends photographs of me with
"lots of hair, just in case you've forgotten
how it was with us, when the world was young."

I am not as old as this kid in camouflage,
yawning before going to war: coffee, then karma,
then quick, quick, another friend gone.

On the TV: the healing powers of aloe vera.

SANTIAGO IN SAN JUAN

The garden is full of flames.
The matchbook is full of roses.

Children borrow binoculars
to spy on their own shadows.

Midnight—you with a black eye—
like you, I've had a few lovers.

They've had me also. Icarus,
you stupid boy, you'll never be

blonde as the sun, blue-boned
like the sea. Let's enjoy the moon.

Sounds of wings in the night:
birds and angels being plucked.

KIKO

Where's my psychic paycheck?
Or love letter with condom enclosed?
I've stripped to my bones in
strangers' bedrooms, forced to be
my own demon lover. I shower.
It's all fucked up and down:
I hide in my house, reading Foucault,
dead of AIDS that he went outside of
his body to seek. How can my
pueblo not be postmodern?
Sí, see: my mailman is a woman!
Señor Andy Garcia is *muy macho*,
but why "Andy" like in that Andy of
Mayberry, RFD? Or "Richard" Rodriguez
instead of Ricardo like Little Ricky's
last name in *I Love Lucy? Hola,*
head full of dreams. Old bills follow me
into a new century like stupid, faithful dogs.

Some Adventures of Juan Angel

1.

Juan Angel is not much of a hero but
he's what I have. His innocence is rare,
what with all these talk shows about the cut-
ting edge peopled by gays, Muslims, thugs, beer
drinkers, weepy evangelists, and the lot.
Some say Juan Angel is slow (anywhere
out of bed that's bad, I guess), but he is
my last hope for some literary prizes.

2.

So I give him a crisis before you're bored.
He found an illustrated version of
Byron's *Don Juan*. It was full of whores
turned nuns. So he asked his priest about love,
something the hairy man in the shower
of the church basement knew about; the gloves
were off. Juan Angel listened to the priest
confess his sins. He set for them a feast.

3.

He learned his body was mysterious,
had a history as old as Adam's.
The boy sunbathed on his roof, curious
as a *Star Search* spokesmodel sans pants.
He traced the Big Dipper and various
constellations without shame. Oh, fuck them
if critics forget their troubled childhoods.
Poor Juan Angel was a wolf without woods.

13

4.

The Widow Sánchez was drying her clothes when
she saw a naked god across the street.
She was poor: no man and no heroin.
She ate rice and beans without salt or meat,
which might explain nothing. What does? She then
went screaming into the night. That's when Juan
Angel learned the power of his body.
He dreamt that night of moons, June, and money.

5.

And when he woke up, he was twenty-one,
legal, and chaste. He wanted to know if
sex was dangerous but as a citizen
of the U.S.A., life came without Cliff
Notes. He walked past hockshops that sold used guns,
knowing nothing of Freud or why dogs sniffed
each other's tails. You save the whales, but I
save Juan Angel from mediocrity.

6.

Forget Greece, country without a hit song.
Screw the Romans (Oh, sorry, I meant that
as an expression but a thought belongs
to the cosmos once it becomes a fact).
This young man's radio was made in Hong
Kong. Rock and Roll saved him from the sad fate
of working at McDonald's or Denny's.
Juan Angel never got tipped in pennies.

7.

He watched hot men and women walk around
like story problems with solutions: him.

Oh, the young are young, but the old do drown
themselves in art, politics, *Bull Durham*
(the movie), not knowing that their head wounds
could heal through love and magic, not those damn
products in drugstores or on the street. Sex
perplexed the young boy, then his turn was next.

8.

Juan Angel became twenty-two, five-foot
eight, size-nine shoes, thirty waist, a Yankee-
Doodle-Dandy boy (Hey, this isn't *Roots*!)
born on the fourth of some July, kinky
hair made soft with champagne shampoo, one tooth
with a cavity. But when he smiled, he
distracted: was he hung or not? How we
are often stuck with unsolved mysteries.

9.

He showed his flesh in his rock band, The Swans
without Leda. Our Juan Angel did strip
to his romantic Calvin Klein shorts, dumb
impersonation of Byron or Pip
in *Great Expectations* if loved by King Kong.
Wet with sweat, he'd flash his one-man love ship.
He'd sing of demon lovers in the sack.
Now, let's go Hollywood and fade to black.

10.

I'd rather write about Juan Angel, but
I will say that what's autobiographical
in this story isn't Juan Angel's butt
or other aspects totally physical.
If I wanted a bestseller, I'd put

the young man's virginity aside, haul
Madonna into her limousine, stop-
ping by Latino studs playing hopscotch.

11.

So, Madonna eyed Juan Angel as he
eyed the chauffeur's cap for cues to the next
costume change. The limousine was pretty.
They only *talked* about the book of sex
because Madonna needed irony.
My friends, limos are so easy to wreck!
Juan Angel was still pure and that's a fact,
since Madonna petted too many pets.

12.

Instead, that one night, he seduced a wife
and a husband, one at a time—see how
important numbers are? A good man's life
is a bore as a movie, so let's now
look in on Juan Angel with his dull knife
being sharpened by Julio whose vows
to his wife were merely theoretical.
She, unfortunately, was heterosexual.

13.

Julio had listened to the Widow
Sánchez describe Juan Angel's purity.
Bad news skates while good news hobbles. Hero
without a war, the young man was worried
walking city streets unprotected. So
he knew Julio had tools and stories.
A switchblade was transformed into a sword.
The N.E.A. won't let me say a word.

14.

Julia, Julio's wife, did become
a Christian after Juan-Angeled. Her mouth
praised God for Eva's tempting of Adam.
She moved up the passions that once were south
and had visions of the saved and the condemned:
the old are often corrupted by youth
and vice versa. Our star got injected.
Let's leave him alone while he's infected.

15.

Forgive me, friends! We're without a virgin!
I sacrificed Juan Angel because the Gods
would take him someday. Author as surgeon,
I separated the man from his nods;
he will not be addicted to the hurt.
Pain to exist, pain to not exist. The mods
think this is a fashion cue, watch them twirl.
Are any of our beds not the real world?

16.

In the bodegas, the whispers were sold
that Juan Angel was available.
But he wasn't. He was looking for his soul
at the movies. Andy Garcia, tall
and pouty, well dressed, slight accent, appalled
him at first, but then he wanted him. Small
comfort of the new *Zorro* on TV,
our hero soon had to escape poverty.

17.

Could he be Cantinflas with sexy hair?
Could he be a Charo impersonator?

(She impersonates herself too well.)
Could he be Valentino? A waiter?
What is the fate of a man who's no heir?
Why does the church hate the masturbator?
See how necessary an author is? I
throw Juan Angel into a bar, The Sty.

18.

The Swans without Leda were playing hot,
but when they got backstage Juan Angel flipped:
he saw himself in a mirror and stopped.
He was a man; he could buy his own whip
if he wanted to. He didn't. A cop
came for his autograph. The band just slipped
out the window, into the night, leaving their
excuses in the tongue of their lead singer.

19.

Raúl, the cop, laughed it off, and so Juan
Angel signed the man's palm with red lipstick.
They looked at each other; what had Fate done?
I interrupt. My hero needs a kick
in the ass. He will not carry a gun,
not even for law and justice. How sick.
Yet Raúl looked good in his uniform.
Who can stay liberal when you feel warm?

20.

Raúl and Juan Angel became friends, but
nothing more. This isn't porn, unless I'm
called the Hispanic D. H. Lawrence. Gut
feeling says, "sing on." So Juan Angel's time
had arrived. Critics found him. Bills did not.

The Swans without Leda were singing mimes!
Soon, they were uptown, in blues clubs, applauded.
Even in bar bathrooms they were lauded.

21.

Then the great Swan of Destiny was plucked!
A band member was found murdered, naked in
church. Then another one. They were all plucked
except Juan Angel, the suspect. His sins
were many but he was no Cain. "I'm fucked,"
he told Raúl over lasagna. They grinned
because their friendship was just platonic.
Each found the other man too exotic.

22.

So Juan Angel went solo and hired
Raúl as his bodyguard (Sure, the author
watches MTV to learn of Desire's
latest marketing schemes and tie-ins). Thor,
Juan Angel's new stage name, soon grew tired
of heavy-metal-rhumba combos. Bored,
the singer became I'm Not Leda and
he played the Mexican accordion.

23.

Oh to go back to your kind and enjoy
their words, foods, dances, curses, saints, rum, shrugs!
Don't worry, Raúl wasn't unemployed.
He got checks from the police to buy drugs
from therapists to become his own boy.
Yes, some Latinos do use legal drugs.
Juan Angel and Raúl threw a party.
Pobrecitos, their pad was too arty.

24.

Los vecinos said los hombres had changed.
Caught between two worlds, the two drunk men left
for a bar that rats avoid when the rains
mask the known world. La Luna was for thieves
Genet wouldn't have sex with. Once again
the two best friends kicked gin right in the grief.
Just when they were feeling good, a go-go
came up: Julia, wife of Julio.

25.

After the show, after the bar's closing,
after the Gulf War that wasn't a war,
after the budget cuts, after quoting
the latest White House suicide note ("Poor
man, yes. D.C. is where they think screwing
is fucking your neighbor's career, where cars
are judged and not one's private parts or member."),
after a visit, they don't remember

26.

what lead Julio to attack them with
a knife. Raúl had left his gun behind
strapped to a piñata to make a myth
of himself to the neighbors. He grabbed wine
bottles and threw them even as jazz riffs
floated through the room. Juan Angel designed
a weapon out of his belt and snap! snap! welts
raised on el loco who suddenly knelt

27.

and cursed God for the birth of Juan Angel!
Julia, who had been locked in her room, jumped out

of her window. Julio said he'd tell:
he killed the band members when he found out
he and his wife were willing to go to hell
to keep Juan Angel a slave. Our hero's mouth
was without words. He turned. Julio grabbed
our hero but instead Raúl was stabbed.

28.

Julio suddenly jumped out of the room's
window. *Rescue 911* was called, as
husband and wife were D.O.A. too soon!
"Raúl don't die or I'll kick your dead ass,"
Juan Angel cried. He ripped his shirt off, wound
it around Raúl's wound. Years since mass,
he went to San Carlos to celebrate
his friend, and he vowed to be celibate.

29.

Which he was until . . . but that's another story.
Raúl had a vision in the hospital;
Buddha told him the secret of glory:
a rock in the river will break or grow dull
unless it sings with the water. Laurie,
the nurse, sponge-bathed him; the moon was full.
Juan Angel felt betrayed, jealous, happy, lost.
What was was and what is will soon be was.

30.

Ok, so my hero's grammar is bad.
His heart wasn't. Juan Angel learned to sing
the blues with an accent. Raúl was glad
(bad rhymes sometimes capture such good feelings!)
his friend was back on stage; he was no fad.

Yet, when Raúl caught Juan Angel kissing
off-stage, off-the-record, often, he turned
away. He wanted adventure! He burned.

31.

Juan Angel's heart was heavier than his
balls. He tired of civilization,
of every party being just show biz,
of himself. No psychiatrist's patient
deserved more thorough analysis
but no mercy for Juan Angel. Fashion
demands the author to be lyrical
even as his hero is hysterical.

SPECTACLE REPLACES HOPE

In Las Cruces, Tomorrow
only strips for tourists.

Marta walks her pet
breasts nowhere special.

Jorge poses like a
Chihuahua guarding its beloved.

The Antichrist
will be here soon.

He will be handsome in
the wardrobe of our blood.

TRIGO

Trigo means *wheat*
in Spanish.
It's also a cousin's
name who killed
his woman's husband.
Trigo, rise from
this mud; perhaps
we do sow
what we weep.
You've learned
much in prison—
for example:
your asshole
is everyone's
escape route
except yours.
This poem is
a window cut
into your cell wall.
Watch through it
for signs of
Spring 2009
when you will
walk free under
the palm trees
once again.

Speedy Gonzales, Jr.

1.

So what? Who cares that Marilyn Monroe look-alikes o.d.?
Marilyn was a year of good wine. *Speedy*, a woman once
called me. I said, you're not Marilyn. I made her cry. I felt
like a rich man, a bastard, Columbus kicking pagan ass.

2.

My mother told me to iron my hair flat like some dumb blond
surfer, like a highway in California long after dark. "Imagine,
hijo," she said, "you speeding the hell out of yourself."

3.

I'm the best man. I try on a tuxedo, wrong size. I take it off.
I'm naked before the groom. I'm his best man but I'm the
better man. Speedy, he laughs, don't be afraid. Of what?
Why not be afraid? I ache when cartoon animals run and their
legs don't carry them away.

VIRGINS AND GHOSTS HAVE NOTHING BETTER TO DO THAN LISTEN TO MY PRAYERS

I go to empty prayer services
before work, wait for lottery

numbers to take form in my mind.
I learned from a lifetime of bosses

not to earn my stormy paycheck.
I end up hiding in the ever-public

bathroom, sitting in a shiny stall,
writing *El Zorro* revenge threats

on the wall, waiting for numbers
to grow solid in my poor skull.

No winning number visits, not yet,
and sometimes I laugh at myself,

at my pants down around my ankles,
at my whistling to wake up La Madre,

at my calling on the dead who
didn't help me when they were alive.

ADIÓS, RAFAEL

This month's calendar recipe:
Jazzy Jambalaya Pasta,

"a Mardi Gras medley of flavor."
A cousin named Junior is dead.

Five cousins are named Junior.
One aunt gives up God for Lent.

"There is no resurrection," she writes.
There is no chile pepper hot enough

to slip into the mouth of the dead
to make them sing, to make them sing.

I fill up the calendar with appointments.
Death has many sons. I'm also a Junior.

INFIDELITIES IN THE TROPICS

Artist with long black hair, man of mountain air in his lungs,
former sponge diver, tourist driver and seducer, loud singer,
bruised drunkard, orchard picker early in the mornings while
the sky's tears are still wet on apples & mangoes & pineapples,
wrestler, nest robber, unstoppable mambo dancer, Mr.
Enhancer, romancer of chants, naked tongue teller, fence
philosopher, weather predictor, eater of cold foods, moody
fisherman,

where is your Eve
tonight?

Count your stars again, mend the holes in your flesh, rest your
restless heart, stop listening for footsteps in dark hallways,

where is your Eve
tonight?

she must understand at last that you have ribs without number.

BREATHING LESSONS

Yet another Puerto Rican
Buddhist. He wants to breathe in
peace, while keeping his rice-
and-beans cooking skills, his accent,

his blue jeans from the Santana
years, his wine and rum collections
housed inside his head. Today's lesson:
fireflies know they're grasshoppers'

illusory stars. And that
Puerto Rico is only
a comma in Time's poem some
have called the Great Antilles.

The word "greater" is too much ego,
an egg which only revolution
can hatch. Fireflies in San Juan
around El Morro are gardens

with feet and wings. He breathes in. In.
It's the breathing out that is
difficult, for it's a loss. Loss
has, in the past, been his source of

knowledge. If he gives that up, then
loss will no longer be a gain, gains.
Meditation is like a game
of monopoly with his

Latino friends. It always ends
with a coup: the upturned board,
hotels thrown into the air,
useless get-out-of-jail cards,

a shower of dollars suddenly
worthless because of the players'
disbeliefs. He feels Puerto Rican
in New York, American

in San Juan, and Catholic
in Buddhist temples. He has blamed
karma for his bad Protestant
lovers. Joy is joy, even if

fleeting, or found when one is
being tortured. Buddha said that.
So did Genet. And Oliver Stone.
So does a fisherman friend who

sleeps with soldiers just to steal their
guns ("In case of an emergency
war!"). He isn't the reincarnation
of Che. He must find other

excuses to breathe below his waist.
A teacher warns aloud: "Forget yourself,
you are wind." Does he want to let go
of memories, that Spanish entrée?

No more codfish, pork feet, chicken
breast stuffed with chick peas and carrots,
steak with baby onions so it is
Venus wearing a pearl necklace.

He sits and waits not to be waiting.
He sits on toilets, sits on busses,
sits at his desk, sits at lunch
counters, sits in a lobby for

the latest physician who
will comfort him ("No, you're not dead").
He sits in the bathtub filled with tears for
an ancient water god long

evaporated into air.
Baptists once told him to trust that
they would pull him out of the deep
end of the baptismal pool by

his Samson-like pubic hair.
He watches MTV's *The Grind* and
sees men and women reject their
childhood by running away with

their hips. His wet dreams drown him.
He wakes up gasping for air. But
Buddha teaches that most beaches
in Puerto Rico are illusions,

that the naked and the dead are
not obscene but opaque. He longs
for *home*. Longing is thinking so
he takes bigger breaths. In, in, in,

out. He is tired of being
the serpent of the Caribbean
in the tequila bottle. He
is no message floating in

the sea. He has nothing to say. He
is nothing. Nothing hurts his lungs. He
lunges into the Void. But he grows
afraid as he has been so many

countless times when his airplanes
began their descents into San Juan,
urban ghost that embraces
him until he too is breathless.

2

THE RED BED

I pack those days in pages
of poems that dare to sing
of lives and deaths: seasons.
—Glenn Sheldon

HOLA, HOLLYWOOD

I was once an extra in a movie about
the Valentine's Day Massacre.

I had to walk down a pretend
street of five buildings,

a whistling delivery boy
from the local taco shop.

When the machine guns started to sing
I dove into the gutter.

I did this for three hours to be
on the screen for three seconds,

a star in the American night.
I ran out of the theater shaking.

I stopped at a Mexican restaurant
and spotted a Puertorriqueño

washing other people's plates
(*what's new about that old news?*)

I taught him a new song: "If wishes
were horses we'd all drive Porches."

I finished my bad eggs and stuffed $5
into the man's pocket of holes.

I raced out of there, back into my life:
still waiting to be reflected in the mirror.

Men and women mistake my red bed
for some enchanted island, for theirs.

I'll always be just a singing shark
in *West Side Story*, an underpaid monster.

IMAGINE THE DEVIL DOING THE TANGO

His thick tail dragging unharmed
through lava. His raw laughter
and his rude phallus. Joy pours
you a cup of cheer. The feet stop
and the talk turns to Haitian
cemetery architecture. No whispering.
Leaves fly back to trees, tongues
on fire with the light of Eternity.
You screw in a bed that turns
to ash even as you turn under Satan's
widening chest. You climb his
tongue back into your life, your
smoking clothes, your cigarette-veiled
morning. Sunday arrives like a shy
firefly and as sincere about lighting
your way but where to? You gather coals,
sticks, papers with legal versions
of your names and launch them into
darkness with just one match.
You jump in, bride of light. Unnamed
demons dance on your bones. Your
flesh is real, real enough to lose
in one burst of flames, one grand
blinding wink with your eyelashes on fire.
Just then Lucifer abandons you.
The ballroom shrinks to the size of
a half-note. What exactly is music?

JUAN ANGEL

Rock & Roll is about work, working at
dreams. Lately I've been trying to visualize
        things. Like attracts like. Like if I
think I might get famous why I'll
        get famous. Juan might become JUAN,
in neon. I'm sure of it. I'm Fame's
        angel. ANGEL. *West Side Story* taught
Puerto Ricans to walk like they're
        suddenly going to explode into . . . a
dance. All Latins are lovers and
        are required by law to be able to mambo
and samba and tango and salsa
        and do any forbidden dance. . . .
It's as if you have to want to become
        Charo or the Spiderwoman who kisses the
American William Hurt to death. Like . . .
        like they couldn't find one unemployed
Latino actor to take over the role!
        Or were they afraid of giving a Hispanic
the Academy Award? Anyway, it's safe.
        And it was Puerto Rican drag queens and
Black drag queens that started
        the Stonewall riots because Judy dared to die.
The hard part of living alone is
        trying to take pictures of yourself.
Not always in drag. It's always a
        close-up unless, of course, your arms
grow unusually long. I love
        pictures! I keep trying to choose
the ones that are going to make the
        best album covers. I told you I'm

trying out this visualizing thing.
      Like thinking myself into record stores.
Like I can see it already:
      Oasis Records and a fan looks up, spots
me. Screams. Fans start chasing
      me. ME! Like what happened to the
Beatles in *A Hard Day's Night.* I'm
      running and running so my fans don't
catch up or lose me either. It's
      a delicate balance. I mean look at
Elvis' ghost. It can't haunt
      Graceland in privacy. God gave me my
privates for a reason. I've been
      practicing! For the video shows. I
not only know how to lip sync,
      I hip sync! I'm good in my empty bed:
              Hello
            I'm blonde
           Goodbye
        I'm brunette
     After two vodkas
   You're easy to forget
        Hey you
         I'm easy
  But man you're sleazy
            Sure
     I want everything
       Everything
    That has a sting
    I have to feel it
    To make it real
    I have to feel it
    I have to feel it

Oh, once I started a band but
all of us wanted to be the star power.
When the neighbors called the cops
we told them we were on *Star Search*.
"Fame! I'm going to live forever."
I'm Juan Angel. I'm keeping my name.
I mean people know Gloria Estefan.
Trini López. Rita Moreno. Julio Iglesias
showed up once on *The Golden Girls*.
My mother was born in the same village
in Puerto Rico as José Feliciano.
A sign! That I'm Juan in a million.
Juan-derful. Juan is the one. Juan toss
of the dice. Juan chance of a lifetime.
Juan-na dance! Gotta dance!
I'm the Juan and only Johnny Angel.
Oh, Johnny, boy, man, Johnny-come-lately.
Out of my way Madonna. I mean, why did
she get the #1 hit, "La Isla Bonita?"
Barry Manilow and that "Copa Cabana."
Father used to sing me to sleep with
"La Bamba." Why didn't I record it first?
I dream big, but no matter how big I
dream I'm smaller than life, smaller.
I'm tired of waiting for the big break,
the big man, the big boys, the big game.
I'm tired of waiting. Reminds me of
that old Spanish joke about us that
while waiting for a new life in
America we're waiting on tables.
I want to be in America. "Born in
the USA." See you on an album cover
near you. I'm Juan Angel. Hola, hello?

My First Novel

There is the sea

a priest steps out of the water as a shark snaps at his shadow

there is the sea
and the burning moon

a drag queen extinguishes the sky with glasses of ice and
blue gin

there is the sea
and a gossiping moon
eying white gravestones

a reporter warns an addict that someone will escape through
his asshole

there is the sea
and a sailor who is without
cigarettes in a cemetery
overgrown with moonlight

a poet stands naked in his green garden grateful to be
growing blind

there is the sea
left to the moon's abuse
while the sailor sleeps

a thief in prison sleeps so much in the sun that he shits gold
coins

there is the sea
and a drowning moon

a student sobs that in the movies the wind can freely enter
                                        any town it wants

there is the sea

a sailor returns to the mermaid who has promised to eat his
                                        heart

there is the sea

there is the sea

there is

here is

here

he

THE IMMIGRANT

I hurt and so I play *West Side Story*
soundtrack 5:51 am.

Death is no one's pet and it's
ridiculous to love Tony, his

optimistic "one-handed catch."
I'm under blankets, under the weather,

under God, under someone else's gun.
"María, María," I'm no opera queen.

Not yet, although I do seek beauty in fiction
far from phone bills, those sad songs.

There Are Ghosts Who

only do cameos, so
Shelley said last night

with his naked white
arms about himself as

I poured champagne. He
taunted me: "Who are

you to complain Señor
Scarecrow? It was a

small bomb that blew
up your car in your driveway.

You kept your skeleton."
For ten days I walked

around in a daze wishing
I had been raised

by Che and not Freud
('Destroyed property implies semen

spent too soon'). Why
have I ignored advice

from that transvestite uncle:
"Never mind putting messages

in bottles. Just take
the shoe off a sudden

sailor, mix a drink
in it, make toasts

to what means most
to you even if

it's just him for one
night." Instead, I read

more poems. Then I
borrow sleep in gin's

dream bed of light.

MY TRANSVESTITE UNCLE IS MISSING

1. *Questions*

I remember you so Elvis Presley-thin
and ever about to join the army (*now I know*

the whys of that), and I remember remembering you:
before breasts, before European wigs, when

the etc. of your sexuality was a secret,
and you babysat me, and we danced to Aretha,

and you taught me to scream for the joy of
a song on the radio ("Romeo requests this from

his grave!"), and I can't call you, what's
your new legal name? Is it in the phone book?

Are you that official? I've heard you're
dead, call me collect please, I'm on my own,

and Uncle Rachel if you were here tonight I'd . . .
I'd sing to you: "Pretty woman walking down

the street of dreams," and you could tell me
that story again where gold is spun out of straw

2. *Answers*

News of your old death, first I danced in the shower with
clothes on, cracked my green head against a corner, gave you a
bloody birth in my mind, gave myself a satisfying scar,

watched an Annie Lennox video where she has a red towel on
her head, I mirrored her, white towel to stop the bleeding
inside my own nest of a skull, then I screamed and screamed,
but the police never came, snow fell from the constellations,
everything was on fire, fast forward, tumbling and I stupidly
read the Song of Solomon for comfort, my eye filled up with
blood, I strapped a big bandage around my head, I'm a poor
man's Wilfred Owen, I'm my own damnation, you're dead,
I won't sing at the funeral that took place without me, the
sun will hear my confessions, my naked body on a rooftop,
cruel cock crowing as if another ordinary morning, and it is,
I did survive, I, someone shows up to make sure I'm not in a
coma, I'm not, not with all these memories, I touch myself as
if I'm still loved, Uncle Rachel, does Death look sexy without
a fig leaf?

TITO

The monied grandmother welcomed his
ugly woman into the family,

swallowed her up during holiday
parties until all that remained

for Tito was an unbared scarecrow.
He was still scared of his desire

for soldiers from Nicaragua living
and loving above him, under God.

The uncles would cluck when
the bride would bend over

and play at putting her
head in the oven, laughing:

"That's the secret of her cooking!"
Tito loved her then, imagined

basting her, dancing sometimes
with her in front of all the others.

He wanted to stop listening for
the sound of boots in the hall.

Still, he listened for it,
followed it upstairs into

rum visits with the soldiers who
told him stories about sleeping naked

in mud to hide from enemy airplanes.
The war inside Tito escalated.

His heart was like a piñata, only
without any of the celebration.

HOME

Glenn's birthday, 1993

It's as if I've come back from the dead,
as if the cement of these days

really hasn't turned me into a statue.
Life without you hasn't been life.

Even this rain feeds only stones;
when are stones ever harvested?

I can't bring you that sun from Land's End,
so many years ago: I remember waking up

in the car; we couldn't afford a hotel.
Yellow in the air was light, only liquid,

waves seeking solid shore to break against.
There was only your face, locked in a dream.

MY REVOLUTIONARY

I can't afford underwear
but then
wearing nothing makes me feel
pensive
like I'm the man in the moon's
bastard.
I will waltz with everyone's widow
and widower.
I crown the dead in the name of
Revolution.
My shadow is the only lover I can
trust.
I'd rather spend my money on
bullets.
I put them in the cupboard
next to
tomato paste, beans, canned foods
from a United
States I can't even picture in
sunlight.

JULIO'S CARIBBEAN

Summer is paralyzed
above the waist.
I'm naked on
a rented rooftop.
Radio talk show:
"Men in comas often
wake up with erections."
Why can't we stay
young forever?
Prescriptions
instead of fortune
cookie messages.
A man-boy impersonates
James Deans'
deadly crotch.
Friends off themselves.
I read Shelley
while tanning,
while toughs circle
an ice-cream truck.

PABLO

Eating at Tijuana Taco,
you come to mind.

How you'd hate the
mushroom taste of this

#7 burrito special.
You lost your faith in Jesus

upon reading that book on mushroom
cults and holy crosses.

You: "How can civilization be based
on a fungus?" Me: "So?"

I didn't know then how young
we were but I do now as

a boy serves me my meal.
Where are you? Who are you?

Does the mushroom shape of
an atomic blast still fill you up

with irony? How we thought
of ourselves as sexy and doomed.

Why I Hate Pittsburgh #2

All these statues to
capitalists that gave money
to libraries, hospitals, retirement
homes for steel workers.

Look, someone has tattooed
Andrew Carnegie's backside with
a heart and two names:
Ricky and Luis, *hermanos*.

Sex happens without a bankroll
or permission, and why check
out a book when
you can check someone's

body in bed? Video
stores push films like
A Room with a View,
Columbus' Erotic Diary,

and *Alejandro Does Arizona*
which are allegories for
screwing the poor so
they like it, want it,

and erect statues to
rich men's erections.

OBITUARY

I haven't been taught how to mourn.
I haven't learned it in schools or in hotel rooms or in bars
        or in funeral homes or in supermarkets or in libraries
        or in laboratories.

Yet here I am mourning a stranger,
Reinaldo Arenas,
yes,
I mourn you.
Who were you?

I never met you,
never felt the weight of your handshake,
never talked about poetry in an espresso bar,
never argued over a check neither one of us could afford to
                                                        pay,
never read more of your books than *Farewell to the Sea*,
never called you Adonis as a way to make fun of your
        unpoetical bed partners,
never told on myself,
never talked about the *Matador Complex* in post-Hemingway
        Caribbean poets.

How can I not be personal with this impersonal stranger?

Who weren't you?

47 years to learn the art of suicide,
for your death to be a punchline:

"Which author killed himself
because he had AIDS

and he was dying
even as his agent Mr. Colchie
was calling to say,
'A rich Cuban exile
who admires your work
has offered to take you to Florida
where you can spend your remaining days'?"

—Yes, name that queer Shakespeare!

Reinaldo
I mourn you.
I have no right to even use your name in this poem.
I have no right to act like a loved one.
I have no right to wake up your spirit to ask it: "Spirit,
        tell me the secret history of mourning in the Americas."

You have left me behind
in a strange country:
this morning I find
three bars of soap
in my mailbox,
samples named *Spirit*.

I plagiarize their cardboard cover:
- 3 In One
- Cleans
- Moisturizes
- Deodorant Protection
- NEW!
- Blue Sample Size
- Not For Resale

How can I not think of coffins?

And I'm tired of the "*re*" words in English:
>*Re*-view, *re*-constitute, *re*-vision, *re*-
>write, *re*-configure, *re*-cite, *re*-claim, *re*-
>coil, *re*-act, *re*-act, *re*-act, *re*-act, *re*-

Present you
in this poem:
>as if your ghost in this inky blackness will ever leave
>physical traces in my red eyes, my burning pages.

I speak English like a record that's stuck on the word *me*:
>the day *I* heard about your death *I* cried in the men's
>bathroom stall, and *I* dried *my* eyes and nose with
>paper too fragile for *my* words.

Graffiti in the church bathroom this morning reads:
>"I'm straight but a blowjob
>is a blowjob unless you meet
>a stranger with a blowtorch."

I think you wrote this,
as a joke and a warning.
You knew that we would meet there, then, here, now.

SORROW

The fire escape can't save you
anymore. I yearn for tulips.

The cat sleeps next to me.
I've been forgiven

whatever crime I committed
three hours ago. Someone

has painted a Nazi
cross on the next-

door building wall. Red.
Blood. Johnny, what runs in

your useless veins now?
A new friend yells back

at the movie *Longtime
Companion*: "Don't let go!"

I said that to you years ago.
You're still real in this poem.

3

EXISTENTIALIST WITH CONGA DRUM

Let no man despise thy youth.
—Timothy 4:12

THE CARLOS POEMS

The first visit

Hello, William Carlos Williams, you've come
calling, at last! Last night, that dream about

you woke me up! We were somewhere—you said,
"Fuck it, break speed limits, blur the landscape."

I remember looking into your mouth. Your
ghostly teeth were glowing like the back of

eucalyptus leaves in a thunderstorm.
But William, how was I supposed to know

that your middle name Carlos meant *Carlos*,
like the name of some cousins? You, the *most*

American of poets according
to critics! You, *amigo*, who upon

seeing the Caribbean for the first
time "wanted to cradle it like a blue

seashell, like any other dumb tourist. . . ."
You were half-Puertorriqueño? Let's take

a walk. Let's walk past the open windows
of undergraduates with shut eyelids.

These poor students have tired themselves out
listening to Belly, Morrissey, Butthole

Surfers, Throwing Muses, Dead Kennedys.
There's a Chicano rapper now, Kid Frost:

no more silence for *la raza* (*Carlos,
that's the people*), for any one of us.

You are one of us if only by blood.
Look, William, you still have a shadow, your

many words on many pages. I love
what you asked me in the dream this morning:

"If you must own an aquarium why not
fill it up with expensive champagne?"

Ah, *amigo*! Already the daylight
chases you away: not yet, *por favor*!

Unhatted as we are, we dare not
walk any further towards what is

on the next block, and the next, and the next.
You smile at me. I make you remember

something: hunger, youth, time, the need to need.
Adiós, goodbye, yes this is right, William

Carlos Williams, *a-diós*, go back to your God.

The second visit

You follow me to a matinee, sit
in the row behind me; funny, *Dead Again*.

Carlito, that's Andy Garcia. I
don't know why he is with rich, white people

without them noticing his lovely brown
skin, his blue-black hair, head shaped like a bell.

He is not trying to pass as white; were you?
You did pass as an American, as the

North American. You did publish as an
American, judged the *Pisan Cantos*

as what an American citizen speaks.
Andy Garcia is fistfighting with

British Kenneth Branaugh over the soul
and the body that comes with it of a

beautiful woman. Was Pygmalion
the inspiration for the Statue

of Liberty? William, alive again,
but so are young lovers here in this dark

theater with us, feeling each other up
as if dreaming with eyes and legs open.

A lover (such a lovely word, *lover*)
said to me: "Is that a revolution

in your pants or are you just happy to
see me?" See how silliness is such an

American patent? Let's go. No, no,
Carlos, this isn't porno. Do you

know the term *blue movie*? Delicious, no?
English, what a magician you are

on good days. Blue movies make me think of blue
bodies: the waving of blue feet, dancing

blue arms, the rubbing of blue chests and breasts,
the kissing of blue hands. It's not like that;

it's never like that. Let us meditate
on popcorn, the seats, shoes, rows, aisles, curtains,

the American flag in the corner,
ushers, spilled Good & Plentys, screen scratches,

exit signs. Andy Garcia is fading.
The movie is over; then, the sudden

ordinary light of the world, our world,
burns with meaning and power. Look at me

talking to a ghost instead of working.
But perhaps this is my work. What is

poetry if it isn't the public
memory of a night wasted singing?

Carlos, to quote Doris Day, *que será,
será. Ser* is the verb *to be*. You were.

I hope to be. How to part from you? Ah,
mi casa es su casa which roughly

translates as *my poem is your poem.*

EXISTENTIALIST WITH CONGA DRUM

1.
I love Desi.
In America, north
of the equator,
his name is Ricky.

Ricky marries a redhead
on black and white TV.
When his son is born
he is in voodoo face.

In the father's
waiting room he is
grabbed by the police
for scaring nurses

with his painted
cannibal teeth.
Little Ricky comes out
of the camera's womb.

2.
The sky falls into
my crib and my skin
isn't as blue as my mouth.
I taste air,
swallow it, float on my
screams toward tomorrow.
Eternity can't crush me.
It's jealous I have form.
I shake my rattle,
God's bones.

3.

Desi hits the drum.
Or is it Ricky?

Hollywood is hungry
for his Cuban bones.

It's not magic he needs.
What he needs isn't business.

4.

Lucy is American
except for her
choice of lovers.
How brave this Mother
of Multiculturalism.
Ricky and Lucy don't think
of their bodies as islands,
but that's what they are
in Hollywood swimming pools.

5.

Lucy refuses to be
the Mother of Heaven.

Ricky weeps until there are
enough pearls for tourists' necks.

Cubans chew sugar cane
on the road after revolution.

Lucy likes to anger Ricky
so he spews Spanish like a volcano.

Time is a terrorist who casually
straps bombs to his testicles.

Before life on Earth, there was death.
Death had nothing at which to laugh.

6.

Lucy is in disguise.
Her breasts hide among plums.
She joins *turistas* with cameras.
Tranquility is lost,
like the waters in the moon's
Sea of Tranquility.
Ooops, wrong sitcom.
Havana glows in the dark
of 1950's United States.

7.

Ricky is an orchestra leader.
Between the legs of his band
are instruments to tame
the beasts of Capitalism.
The white patrons dance in white
tuxedos surrounded by white orchids.
Ricky can't lose his accent or
Havana will wilt in his·mouth.
He is a crooner, moon-scarred lover.
This Castro-fleeing cocksman,
defrocked jock, is forced
to take up sing-song in Miami.
He marries Technicolor Tess
of the d'Urbervilles
a.k.a. Miss Liberty.

They become lovers, naked
in the minds of suburbs,
trailer parks, and gossip columns.
He has the goods: Desi
desires a destiny
and he is damned with one.
He can't keep his pants on,
swimming in beds, trying
to escape shark after shark.
He has never left Cuba.
The FBI wants him to kill Castro.
Cuba's Casanova hasn't diddled
Hoover, who is enraged that Castro
stares into America's loincloth.

8.

Lucy hums "Happy Birthday"
to herself hoping
to break strangers'
hearts and piggybanks.

9.

No Latinos play Little Ricky.
He takes after Lucy.

She is white and red,
like a cool drink in any Hilton.

The son of the television gods
is attractive, the way

a wreck attracts strangers
and the strange media.

Maybe I'm not Little Ricky.
Maybe Reinaldo Arenas was.

He was just like Big Ricky:
fucking, fucking, fucking.

Pleasure is a strange god.
It rejects familiarity.

Ricky with Reinaldo as a son
could have turned constellations

into strip shows, something
for every sex and species.

The ache to love too often proves
to be just an ache, an acre of air.

Reinaldo, return to your novels
and to your rat-poison suicide.

I wept upon hearing of it, that
you left me as heir to Nothing.

Cuba, don't stop being real:
But then Art makes as many promises as it has holes. . . .

10.

Lucy goes to her first
Catholic church.
She picks up a saint's bone
and pretends she is

the baton queen of New York.
She puts the bone
against her nose.
Now she's a cannibal!

How cute! She is a physical
actress! No confessions for her!
Scriptwriters follow her
to the end of the 20th century.

11.

An *I Love Lucy* TV marathon.
This life's karma tires me out,
but it's Valentine's Day morning.
The cat pisses in her private boxed beach.
God, send me a blue jay, or UFO.
Or any sign, signal, signed studio photo.
I'm tired of painting myself nude,
as if my nudity is the mystery.

12.

This room is bone white,
foam white, Ricky-Ricardo-teeth white,
Moby-Dick-the-sperm-whale white,
Claude-Van-Damme's-stomach white.
He's sexy, in a neo-colonial butch way.
This is a new world of snow, peopled
by snowmen who can't salsa:
"I refuse to limbo under zero degree's line."
Queer to quote myself. Charles Henri Ford
did the same thing during my visit to his
dark Dakota apartment. Indra served us tea
before taking our pictures, turning us

into statues without a garden.
Like Ricky, we live in constant exile.
A republican tells me that there is nothing
romantic about Cuba so long as Castro
blows Gabriel's horn out of his asshole.
He imagines southern Florida as a nest of
killer bees, blue with the hunger for home.
Anne 2 reads Foucault ("Not for fun").
On the TV, Desi and Lucy pretend to be
Ricky and Lucy. He covers his ears
so he doesn't hear his wife mother him.
The laugh track can't be translated.
It's white noise, only darker.

13.

I'm an existentialist with conga drum
tom-tum tom-tum tom-tum
tom-tum tom-tum tom-tum

I love Lucy now isn't that fun?
tom-tum tom-tum tom-tum
tom-tum tom-tum tom-tum

The earth is old but I am young
tom-tum tom-tum tom-tum
tom-tum tom-tum tom-tum

Revolution doesn't need gum
tom-tum tom-tum tom-tum
tom-tum tom-tum tom-tum

The hanged man dances like he's hung
tom-tum tom-tum tom-tum
tom-tum tom-tum tom-tum

Lovers, conga before you're undone
tom-tum tom-tum tom-tum
tom-tum tom-tum tom-tum
tom-tum tom-tum tom
tom-tum tom-tum
tom-tum
tum
tu
t

THE FIELD

This field of snow is
       like an angel's hairless
stomach. Funny how
       perfection always hurts
my eyes. I learned
       in Sunday school that
Moses turned away from
       his one chance to see
God, face to face, man
       to Superman. I was a boy
when Mother sent us to
       the German church a block away
from our house on George
       Street because of two reasons:
1. Surely, Jesus would guard
       His own children from a gang
like the Latin Lords.
       2. And besides, the people who
walked into that church
       looked so clean, so sinless.
Even when Mother saw
       documentaries of naked,
dead Jews in snow she
       couldn't blame Germans:
"Hitler was a hypnotist."
       Of course, that was during
the time when hypnotism
       wasn't a science but
something that happened on *Popeye*
       so Olive Oyl could walk

across steel girders
  in the sky without being
afraid for her life.
  I grew up afraid of death.
It's not really dark
  in any field filled with
snow, for there is that glow,
  that eeriness of a theater
where a silent, black-and-
  white film is playing.
What comes to mind is
  Mrs. Rudolph Valentino's
Salome. Scratchy, old film.
  So that when John the Baptist's
head is presented on a platter
  like dessert, I'm assured that
horror lives in the past as if
  it never really happened, or
it happened on a sound stage
  before a deaf camera. Also
silent is the land under
  snow, silent about what it was
when it was just a field
  offering us its flowers
that we cut and placed
  on our dinner table.
The angels in my Bible ate
  birdfood, seeds I'd just throw
into the wind. Gravity was
  just as hungry as heaven was.
Mother stopped sending me
  to church because of my nightmares
of being swallowed alive
  by Jonah's whale in the sky.

I was sure snow was foam from
          his unholy blowhole, that I
had already been eaten and swallowed,
          that I was already inside his cosmic
stomach. I needed comforting.
          I still do.   I feel this displaced
when I'm in the middle of a field
          of snow, with whiteness ahead
and behind me. Again, I'm the dark thing,
          the dreamer when not in a dream.

The Singing Shark Dream, or Toto, I Don't Think We're in Tegucigalpa Anymore

I'm a shark
    no, not a metaphor
        no, not an allegory
I'm a shark
Doubt it?
Put your hand near my mouth and gain
    a belief the hard way
I'm María's &
 Tony's son, born after *West Side Story*
        became another Hollywood story
my father was once a Shark lover
a gang member
—his, a theatrical choice
          y Mami?
she was a Puertorriqueña
famous for
    wearing a white dress to a dance
        oh, spotlight of purity to
           the itchy stomping white boys
well, one, Papi,
    if he and Mami had finished
        high school before it finished them
           before reading *Romeo & Juliet*
           before living & dying it
why they'd get the hell out of heavenly Nueva York
go through the Lincoln Tunnel
    (the United States' asshole:
        "everything and everyone passes through it")
           We, the other sharks, the sons and
           daughters of other tragedies—what you

think, I'm all alone? There are lots of
other half-humans and half-sharks—we
don't like poetry but root for Mami and
Papi everytime I tell their story, a three-
hour dance, a three-hour dance. . . .
Mami never told her Tony
she got pregnant and it was too late
    to do that because Papi was one
        beached, stinking Shark-loving Jet on
            that infamous basketball court
Mami went mad
    Manhattan turned into Puerto Rico
her rich port of suddenly
    unimportant poverty
how Mami María grieved
    for her dead
shark-hungry lover and so I
    slowly took the shape of
her memories in her womb
    and when the doctors
pulled me out of Mami's
    body they first saw
my back fins and dropped me
    into a water cooler
so I thought Earth was
    bluer than it was on the outside
I was smuggled out of
    the hospital and hidden in
the Central Park Zoo
    how clever to hide someone like me
among sharks among my kind
    but they THEY tHeY ThEy TheY they forgot
        I'm human, that I can remember some
            of what is memorable

78

so Papi is a dead jet
crashed airplane
hijacked hard-on
and Mami redecorates her breakdown
                    I send her a message:
                    a big aquarium for me, please
        So I watched white children
    in children carriages
being children
to their parents
and they learned to walk
and I learned to walk
in my mind at first
                    stumble after st-
                                umble
            I did walk after closing time at the zoo:
                    María's and Tony's freak son on two fins
not so strange
since humans
did swim out
of the sea
and learned
how to stop
gasping
beyond foam,
beyond waves,
beyond the wetness
of the pleasure
of being
        so Mami was my cosmic shortcut in evolution:
                    hey, I'm with the band
I'm a shark
    with a man's mind ever so hungry, ever with
an ancient eye fixed

on God and Satan,
            skinny snacks, my motto is
            have teeth, will travel
Oh
yeah
I
can
sing
1. La: a note that follows So, or La: def. art. fe. sing. the.
2. La: obj. pron. her; it; you. 3. La: m. MUS. la, A.
                        Think of my parents
                    where I come from
                            Think the rhythm of water
against my brain at birth
                        and since
while learning to walk I listened to sounds around me,
guarding against night guards, I heard car radios, televisions,
jukeboxes with bars, drunks whistling, televisions, walkmen,
walkwomen, commercials in the air, surfers rehearsing
commercial cues, Zorro vs. the Energizer bunny, shoe
songs, slow heartbeats
                        I can sing
                        I can dance
                        I can be funded:
                        Anger
                    just leave it on the hanger
                    no, I'm not angry anymore
                        danger
                    don't pick up the stranger
                        Baby let's f__k
                        then let's rock
                            to sleep
                    I'm the dream that you can keep
                        I'll rock you to sleep

all night long
this is our song
Baby let's f__k
then let's rock
rock
rock to sleep
You're the dream I can keep
Does the N.E.A. know its ABCs yet?

F is forest
U is utility
C is for clock
K is comely comic
U is for unity
Hello MTV this is your singing shark
son of Tony and María
you know other sons and daughters who sing their way into
identity
I like what Tina Turner says about the movie based on her life:
"I lived it so why see it again?"
That's how I feel
about *Jaws*
West Side Story is a video of my parents'
honeymoon
or lack of one
I'm always aware of *absence*
—isn't that a way to define hunger?
I'm not human
I'm not shark
I'm not a moral lesson
although maybe there is a poem
waiting for you with your name
inside my ancient mouth but beware

snap snap says the Mambo Mouth and RuPaul
and Mami snapped
                and jumped off
                Hart Crane's Brooklyn
                Bridge so she could
                remember what she had
                forgotten and I lead
                a fish guard all the way
                until she sank at the
                bottom of the Earth
                and her hair waved in
                the water like a mirage
                but it was her as I should
                know having come from
                inside her and so Tony
                and María are happy without me
                again and I swim away because
                what else is a shark-boy born to do?
Eve
        was
                buried
                        in
                            the
                                Red
                                    Sea
                                        and
                                                her
                                        blood
                                    makes
                                it
                        red
        —great wave!

82

I'll be on tomorrow's *Oprah* or Telemundo, I can only write
an autobiography on water or on gin, no, I don't expect a
musical based on my life, I'm a Puertorriqueño without
perspective, I'm no *Grease II*, so what is life and death about
as a shark, not so different from your life and death, food and
sex, sex and food, needs, interview me and I will just say: *yo
tengo una tía que toca la guitarra,* although I have no aunt
and no guitar, I'm blowing you off without tasting you, swim
away from me boys and girls, I'll be a television series soon
enough, *seaQuest.* I'm one of the unloved, made during
lovemaking, but some bodies have dark waters in them so I'm
a singing shark without confidence that my future killers will
follow the musical's etiquette: sing before killing, I expect my
freak birth to lead to my freak death, humans love the
parenthesis and doors and illicit affairs, *en voz alta,* I'm on
low cruise speed, but what if I'm not, what if I'm what you
waited for,
la voz del mar nunca se pone vieja,
                              or old sea, new waves
Oh Mami and Papi,
I'm a musical without a hit song:
you, and you, and me (No *Tea for Two* is it?)
     but you're not here
          but you almost are
               you have salty margaritas because you can't sink
I drink Bloody Marys because I can't pray
     how lovely to be stupidly drunk and mean what
you say: my heart is a piñata,
          I'm a shark,
          both things are true,
     I'm thirsty for simplicity:
          Life, you sing to me!